READ ALL THESE

NATE THE GREAT

DETECTIVE STORIES

BY MARJORIE WEINMAN SHARMAT

WITH ILLUSTRATIONS BY MARC SIMONT
(unless otherwise noted)

NATE THE GREAT
NATE THE GREAT GOES UNDERCOVER
NATE THE GREAT AND THE LOST LIST
NATE THE GREAT AND THE PHONY CLUE
NATE THE GREAT AND THE STICKY CASE
NATE THE GREAT AND THE MISSING KEY
NATE THE GREAT AND THE SNOWY TRAIL
NATE THE GREAT AND THE FISHY PRIZE
NATE THE GREAT STALKS STUPIDWEED
NATE THE GREAT AND THE BORING BEACH BAG
NATE THE GREAT GOES DOWN IN THE DUMPS
NATE THE GREAT AND THE HALLOWEEN HUNT
NATE THE GREAT AND THE MUSICAL NOTE
(by Marjorie Weinman Sharmat and Craig Sharmat)
NATE THE GREAT AND THE STOLEN BASE
NATE THE GREAT AND THE PILLOWCASE
(by Marjorie Weinman Sharmat and Rosalind Weinman)
NATE THE GREAT AND THE MUSHY VALENTINE
NATE THE GREAT AND THE TARDY TORTOISE
(by Marjorie Weinman Sharmat and Craig Sharmat)
NATE THE GREAT AND THE CRUNCHY CHRISTMAS
(by Marjorie Weinman Sharmat and Craig Sharmat)
NATE THE GREAT SAVES THE KING OF SWEDEN
NATE THE GREAT AND ME: THE CASE OF THE FLEEING FANG
NATE THE GREAT AND THE MONSTER MESS
(illustrated by Martha Weston)
NATE THE GREAT, SAN FRANCISCO DETECTIVE
(by Marjorie Weinman Sharmat and Mitchell Sharmat;
illustrated by Martha Weston)

Nate the Great
SAN FRANCISCO DETECTIVE

by Marjorie Weinman Sharmat
and Mitchell Sharmat

illustrated by Martha Weston
in the style of Marc Simont

Delacorte Press

PARKER HILL

SPECIAL GUEST APPEARANCES BY
Olivia Sharp, Willie the Chauffeur, and Duncan

from the Olivia Sharp, Agent for Secrets series
by Marjorie and Mitchell Sharmat

Published by
Delacorte Press
an imprint of
Random House Children's Books
1540 Broadway
New York, New York 10036

Visit us on the Web! www.randomhouse.com/kids
Educators and librarians, for a variety of teaching tools, visit us at
www.randomhouse.com/teachers

Library of Congress Cataloging-in-Publication Data

Sharmat, Marjorie Weinman
  Nate the Great, San Francisco Detective / by Marjorie Weinman Sharmat and
Mitchell Sharmat ; illustrations by Martha Weston in the style of Marc Simont.
    p. cm.
  Summary: Nate the Great goes to San Francisco where he solves a mystery for his
cousin Olivia Sharp, who is also a detective.
  ISBN: 0-385-32605-X   ISBN: 0-385-90000-7 (GLB)
  [1. Lost and found possessions Fiction.   2. Mystery and detective stories.]
  I. Sharmat, Mitchell.   II. Weston, Martha, ill.   III. Title.
PZ7.S5299Nawp   2000   99-41493
[Fic]—dc21   CIP

acc
4/00

The text of this book is set in 18-point Goudy Old Style.
Manufactured in the United States of America
September 2000
10 9 8 7 6 5 4 3 2 1
BVG

For our granddaughter
Madeline Lucille Sharmat
with much love
—M.W.S.

—M.S.

For the Shopoffs,
my San Francisco family
—M.W.

CHAPTER ONE
MR. GREAT

My name is Nate the Great.
I am a detective.
My dog, Sludge, is a detective too.
This morning Sludge and I were
at the airport in San Francisco.
We were supposed to meet
another detective there
at ten o'clock.
My cousin, Olivia Sharp.
Olivia always wears a boa
made of feathers.
This makes her easy to find.
Anywhere.
But all we saw were strangers.
And many people with signs.

All at once, I, Nate the Great,
saw a sign that said
NATE THE GREAT
in big letters.
A man in uniform was holding it.
He came up to us.
"Mr. Great and Sludge?" he said.
"I'm Willie. Miss Olivia's chauffeur.
She's out on her eight o'clock case.
It's running late.
She hasn't even started
her nine o'clock."
Willie picked up my suitcase.

"Your limo is over there," he said.
"My limo?"
"Yes. Miss Olivia always
travels in a limo.
But today she saved it for you."
I, Nate the Great, had never
been in a limo.
Sludge had never been in a limo.
It was long and shiny.
We got inside.
Willie got in the front seat.
And we were off.

CHAPTER TWO
CALLING NATE THE GREAT

We drove up and down many hills.
"Is everything all right
back there, Mr. Great?" Willie asked.
I looked at Sludge.
He wagged his tail.
"Fine," I said.

10

"But can you tell me about the case
that's making Olivia late?"
"Her friend Duncan
lost a joke book," Willie said.
"Miss Olivia is looking for it."
Willie drove us to Olivia's house
and let us in.
A telephone was ringing.
And ringing.
This was a phone that
needed to be answered.

"Nate the Great for Olivia Sharp,"
I said.
"Hello, Nate."
It was Annie, from back home.
"We all miss you," she said.
"And Fang has something to tell you."
I heard heavy breathing.
I knew that Annie's dog, Fang,
was on the line.
I was happy to be many miles away
from his teeth.

I waited.

Fang had nothing else to say.

Then I heard a strange voice.

It belonged to Rosamond.

"My turn. Bring back California fish

for my cats. Lots of fish.

All the fish you can carry.

Over and out."

"I thank all of you

for the call," I said.

Then I heard another voice.

"Wait! It's me, Claude.

I lost something."

Claude was always losing something.

"I lost an itsy bitsy seashell

two years ago

on the Golden Gate Bridge.

Find it!"

Claude hung up.

CHAPTER THREE
THE END
OF THE WORLD

The telephone rang again.
"Nate the Great for Olivia Sharp,"
I said.
"Hello. This is Duncan.
It's eleven o'clock
and the world is coming to an end."
I, Nate the Great, hoped that
this Duncan person did not have
his information straight.

14

"I need Olivia," Duncan said.

"Olivia is out," I said.

Duncan moaned.

"Then the world
is really coming to an end."

"Could you be more specific?" I asked.

"Well," said Duncan,
"I lost my joke book.
I have to tell a joke
to a friend at two o'clock
and I forget how it ends."
"Olivia is on your case," I said.
"Yes, I'm her case number twenty-two,"
Duncan said.
"But she is also working on cases
number eighteen and number
twenty-one at the same time.
She'll never solve mine
by two o'clock."
I, Nate the Great, had never
heard such a sad voice.
"Very well," I said. "I will also
take your case."
I hung up.
Then I called my mother.

The answering machine came on.
I said,

"Dear Mother, Sludge and I are on a California case. But it has something to do with the entire world. Or the end of it. Something like that. I will be back. Love, Nate the Great."

CHAPTER FOUR
JOKE STEW

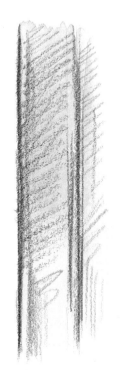

Willie drove Sludge and me
to Duncan's house.
"I will wait in the limo," Willie said.
I knocked on Duncan's door.
He answered it.
Duncan looked even sadder
than he sounded.

His hair was hanging limp,
his socks were drooping,
and his jeans were slipping.
Sludge and I walked inside.
"I am Nate the Great," I said.
"And this is my assistant, Sludge.
Tell us about your joke book."
"Well, I was in Booksie's Bookstore
yesterday," Duncan said.
"I saw this small book
called *Joke Stew*.
It was the only copy there.
I bought it.
I left the bookstore
with the book in a Booksie's bag."
"Then what did you do?"
"I went to lots of other stores
and bought things.
Then I went to Perry's Pancake House."

"A *pancake* house? Good thinking."
"Yes, Perry's Pancake House has
this big, big menu with five pages
of different kinds of pancakes.
I started to read the menu.
The waiter came by.
I ordered mushyberry pancakes.
The waiter left.
I kept reading the menu.
Then I took out my joke book
to find the perfect joke
to tell today.
I found it."

"Then what happened?"

"The waiter brought the pancakes."

"Did you put the joke book
back in its bag?"

"I don't remember," Dunc- ~~~ .d.

"Because something bad happened."

"What happened?" I asked.

Duncan looked down at his feet.

"I can't tell you."

"What *can* you tell me?"

"The world is coming to an end."

I, Nate the Great, wished this case
were coming to an end.
I said, "So the last place
you saw your joke book
was in the pancake house?"
"Yes."
"It might still be there," I said.
I, Nate the Great,
was sure of one thing.
Pancakes were still there.
Five pages of pancakes to choose from!
"I will be back," I said.

CHAPTER FIVE
STICKY, ICKY MESS

Willie drove Sludge and me to
Perry's Pancake House.
"Sniff around outside, Sludge," I said.
"Look for the joke book."
"I'll help Sludge," Willie said.
I went inside the pancake house.
It looked good, it smelled good.

I walked up to a waiter.

"I am looking for a small joke book
titled *Joke Stew*," I said.

The waiter looked mad.

"A girl was just here
looking for it," he said.

"She was wrapped in feathers.
Said she was a detective.
She put up LOST JOKE BOOK signs
everywhere.

Here. There. Up and down the street.
But we have no joke book.

I know who lost it.
Yesterday this boy came in.
I served him mushyberry pancakes.
He knocked the syrup bottle
over everything.
The pancakes, the menu, the table.
Ugh!

I scooped up all the sticky stuff
and dumped it in a bag.
I handed the bag to him.
I told him that somewhere out there
a hungry family of ants or flies
would love this sticky, icky mess."
The waiter was getting madder.
I, Nate the Great, knew that I
had to leave the pancake house
without eating.
I did not want to do that.
But I went outside.
Sludge and Willie were standing there.
"We didn't find the joke book," Willie said.

"We looked in front.
Then Sludge went out back.
He found garbage cans.
He looked in them.
Isn't that the wrong place to look
for a joke book?"

"Well, a good detective knows
that sometimes the wrong place
is the right place," I said.
"Smart dog," Willie said.
Willie, Sludge, and I got into the limo.

CHAPTER SIX
THE GOLDEN GATE CLUE

I liked this limo.
It was a good place to think
and to drive around
to see San Francisco.
I, Nate the Great, was thinking.
I was not having any luck
with Duncan's case.
I had not found his joke book.
I had not found Claude's seashell either.
Perhaps that was because
I had not looked for it.
"To the Golden Gate Bridge,
please," I said to Willie.
"A fine bridge, Mr. Great," Willie said.

When we got there,
Sludge and I peered out the window.
The Golden Gate Bridge
was very, very big.

Claude's seashell was
very, very small.
This was not going to help Claude.
But suddenly I, Nate the Great,
knew that it might help Duncan!
"I have a Golden Gate clue,"
I said to Willie.
"Onward to Duncan's house!"

CHAPTER SEVEN
FROZEN PANCAKES!

Duncan was waiting for us.
"I know all about the spilled syrup,"
I said. "What did you do with the bag
the waiter gave you?"
"I put it in the freezer," Duncan said.
"I like frozen pancakes."
"Did you open the bag first?"
"No, it was too icky and sticky."

I put my hand on Duncan's shoulder.
"I, Nate the Great, know
where your joke book is.
It is in your freezer!"
"Oh, cool!" Duncan said.
Was that a joke?
Never mind.
"I, Nate the Great, say
you were reading the menu.
But you were also reading your joke book.
The menu was big. The book was small.
So the book must have slid
or fallen into the pages of the menu.
Before or while the syrup spilled.
The waiter scooped everything up fast
and put it all in a take-out bag."
"You are a good detective," Duncan said.
"Even if you don't put up signs."

"No problem," I said.

"Olivia has her way. I have mine."

I opened the freezer.

I saw the bag.

I took it out.

I opened it.

It was full of cold, crusty, icky things.

Pancakes, napkins, the top

from a syrup container,

a little tub of butter,

a huge menu . . .

but no joke book!

"The joke book isn't here," I said.

"The world is definitely
coming to an end, correct?"

Duncan looked down at his feet.

"Correct," he said. "I need my book
at two o'clock. And it's after twelve now."

"Do not lose hope," I said.

"That is the worst thing to lose."

I sat down.

"I, Nate the Great, need pancakes.
Sludge needs a bone.

They help us think."

"Have a frozen pancake," Duncan said.

"Thaw it," I said.

"I don't thaw," Duncan said.

"Very well," I said.

"A frozen pancake is
better than no pancake at all.
But give Sludge a nice bone."

CHAPTER EIGHT
LOST IN THE BIG CITY

I ate a frozen mushyberry pancake.
It did not help me think.
Except about my cold teeth.
"What happened after you left
the pancake house?" I asked.

"Well, I had lots of bags.
I dropped them outside
the pancake house.
Then I picked them up
and brought them home.
I put the pancake bag in the freezer
and the other bags over there
in that corner.
But the Booksie's bag isn't there."
"Hmmm," I said.
I went over to the corner
and looked inside all the bags.
No book.
"Both the book *and* the Booksie's bag
are missing," I said.
"I, Nate the Great, say
that we should go
to Booksie's Bookstore.

I think you dropped your book
in its bag when you were
in front of the pancake house.
It wasn't there today.
Perhaps somebody found it
and took it back to the store."
Duncan kept looking at his feet.
"Somebody could have found it
and taken it home," he said.
"Or taken it on a trip.
Or mailed it. Or kicked it.
Anything! This is a big city.
My joke book could be anywhere!"
"You are right," I said.
"I *am?*"
"Yes. This is a big-city case.
Your book *could* be anywhere.
But we don't have enough time
to look everywhere.

So I, Nate the Great,
have to *choose* where to look.
And because the book was probably in
the Booksie's bag when you lost it,
I choose Booksie's Bookstore."
"Oh," Duncan said. "There
is more to this detective
business than I thought."

CHAPTER NINE
WHAT'S WRONG IS RIGHT

Willie drove Duncan, Sludge, and me
to Booksie's Bookstore.
He waited outside with Sludge.
Duncan and I went inside.
"Are books returned here?"
I asked a lady behind the counter.

"Yes."
"Was a joke book returned today
or yesterday?"
"You're the second person to ask,"
the lady said. "A girl with a feather boa
and a bunch of signs
was just asking the same question.
I told her a mystery book
had been returned.
And a children's book,
a cookbook, and a science book.
But no joke book."

"What happens when a book
is brought back?" I asked.
"We put it on the shelf again," she said.
Duncan and I walked away.
"Show me the joke book department,"
I said.
"Why? It won't be there," Duncan said.
"We can't be positive," I said.

Duncan led the way.
"Here," Duncan said. "This is
the exact place I found the book."
I looked around.
I looked hard.
The book *wasn't* there.
"You did not choose
the right place in the city
to look," Duncan said.

I, Nate the Great, already knew that.
I saw Sludge peering
through the front window.
Sludge had not been much help
on this case.
Or had he?
He had looked in the wrong place
for the joke book.
But he knew that
sometimes the wrong place
is the right place.
The wrong place!
"Follow me," I said to Duncan.
I rushed up and down aisles.
At last I came to the place
I was looking for.
The wrong place.
I waved to Sludge.
He wagged his tail.

Then I looked up and down
and across shelves.
And there it was!
Duncan's joke book.
Joke Stew!!!
I took it down
and handed it to Duncan.
"My book! My book!" he said.
"But this is the cookbook section.
Why is my book *here*?"

"I, Nate the Great,
say that the lady told us
a cookbook had been returned.
Whoever put your book
back on the shelf
thought it was a cookbook.
With a name like *Joke Stew*,
it could be."
Duncan smiled. He *smiled*.
I knew the world was safe for now.

CHAPTER TEN
A FEATHERY HUG

Duncan skipped off.

Suddenly I heard a voice.

"You solved my case number twenty-two!"

A bunch of feathers hugged me.

It was Olivia. In person.

"I owe you one," she said.

"Let me know if I can ever
solve a case for you. Any case.
Big, small, easy, hard."

"I think I have something
for you right now," I said.
"It's big and it's small
and possibly it's hopeless.
Willie can take us to it."
I, Nate the Great,
enjoyed the ride
back to the Golden Gate Bridge.

H/001

27,

PARKER HILL